Before The Weaver

A Timberhaven Collection

Aaron Conaway

Aaron Conaway

A K&Q Press Publication

Front Cover Photo Credit: Lauren Conaway

First Edition 2018

3

Books by K&Q Press

The Timberhaven Chronicles

Before the Weaver

Waking the Weaver

Monsters in the Park (Coming Spring 2019!)

The Michael Gideon Collection

I Live Here Now

Spookhunt

Tales for Halloween (Coming October 2018!)

Table of Contents

<u>Preface</u>

Some people have asked me since *Waking the Weaver* came out if I based Timberhaven on a real place in the Midwest. I can tell you, I did. Two small towns in Missouri, actually, though, while some of you have figured out where already, I won't name those towns here.

Maybe another time.

No, this is strictly Timberhaven's spotlight, and between you and me there's a lot to see within that light. Nooks and crannies in need of exploring, so have at them.

If you've read *Waking the Weaver,* you'll have already met some of the cast ahead. Walk warmly along the streets; you know the way. Say hello to any new faces.

Speaking of, if you've not yet read *Waking the Weaver*, no worries. Welcome and pleased to meet you just the same. Everything that happens in this book took place before the events in that one, hence the title, so you're all set.

Only, keep your wits about you while in Timberhaven, yeah? Let this book serve as helpful tour guide of sorts, a map about town showcasing the ins and outs of life here in Timberhaven. The rules of conduct, as it were. It might help you piece together some clues to the riddles of Timberhaven. However, it might just as well further the mystery.

A big Thank You to everyone who has shared so many kind words to me as I continue this adventure, both from the fans of Timberhaven and those friends and family in my life who have always been in my corner. I'll keep telling stories so long as you're there.

I told myself that if I hit a particular goal with *Waking the Weaver* that I'd do something special. I met that goal, exceeded it, actually, and what I came up with was putting this book together.

Hope you enjoy.

A.C.

<u>On a Message Board In Old Town</u>

Welcome to Timberhaven!

Last bastion of Wonder before the idle plains of preparedness.

Some things to ponder as you wander our fair thoroughfares:

One rarely finds loose change on the streets of town; like maybe

there's a horde of misplaced pennies, nickels, and dimes

someplace, gathered beneath the mighty posterior of a fantastical

beast.

Distrust any new songs you hear on Tuesdays, for these are most

assuredly the lamentations of forgotten gods who might regard

your humming along as an invitation to share accommodations.

Proper placement of spoons upon the dinner table keeps the salt

shaker upright.

Figments -- those alterers of opinion, mood, and perception --

oftentimes dwell beneath that last sip of bottled booze.

And finally, mind the stories; for they're all true and they'll

mind you. You'll be fine if your wits are kept.

Clever AND kind is the winning hand.

See you around town.

<u>Alias</u>

It's important to note that Dorian had come into this world born of another. He hadn't asked to be. In truth, he was decidedly against the idea from the off.

Nevertheless.

Any benefit to this new casting he'd found himself in was lost on him. The smells were stronger here, pungent to his aristocratic sensibilities, and the colors sharper still. Almost painful.

And then there was The Master.

Dorian hadn't known such a life of hardship existed until he met The Master. His hands ached from the destruction they wrought under The Master's whip; his soul, diseased as it was, became increasingly maligned under The Master's tutelage.

But secrets he discovered as well.

Such secrets laid in wait in the small village of Timberhaven in the spring of 1945. The Master had succeeded for decades in keeping the truth from Dorian, but the theater would once again offer redemption – or at the least show Dorian the path toward it – and this time he would not be found wanting.

Dorian purchased his ticket and entered the theater. He'd grown accustomed to the moving pictures over the ages, but they'd never held much in the way of enticement for him. That is until he saw his life's journey – his previous life – up there on the silver screen.

Dorian did not care for the man who was playing him – one Hurd Hatfield. But the woman – Angela Lansbury the end credits read – she caused an immense pang of guilt from beneath Dorian's breast, a feeling that until that moment he thought himself incapable.

Sybil.

And thus his plan began to take shape. He'd learned enough while working for The Master that it was possible, this idea he'd conceived, if not overly simplistic. But he would start straight away. Life from beneath the horror of The Master and the beginning of yet another life. Of atonement. He would bring her here just as he had been. They could live the life they missed. It would take careful planning, of course, and they'd need to remake themselves anew in this world, to stay hidden from The Master.

Smythe was a common enough surname here, Dorian thought. Yes. Hurd and Angela Smythe.

And thus Timberhaven would have two new residents within a fortnight.

But that is a tale for another time.

The Junkyard Prince

Juniper Soot is eight-years-old and lives in a junkyard just outside of town. It's not her actual home, you see, but rather where she *prefers* to spend her free time, for reasons that are not the business of you or me.

On Friday she stopped at the gas station for a pack of Pep-O-Mints and a Cherry Coke. The clerk was watching a little T.V. under a shelf. Juniper put her small purse up on the counter. Looking up, the clerk turned off his T.V.

"Pennies again?" he asked, annoyed. "Why don't you ever have any real money?"

"Pennies are coins," Juniper told him. "Coins are money." She continued to count out the pennies until she had paid him. "Thank you!" Juniper opened her Pep-O-Mints and started crunching them on her way out.

When Juniper got to the junkyard, she saw a brown cat waiting just outside the gate, watching her as she approached.

"Hello there," Juniper said, holding her hand toward the cat.

"Hello," the cat said in return.

"What's your name?" Juniper asked seemingly unimpressed with a talking cat as the cat nuzzled her open hand.

"I'm known as Story. I've been invited to a party just inside here."

"You know Sir Bannendworp?" Juniper asked as the two made their way through the gates and deeper into the junkyard.

"Indeed," the cat named Story purred, "though I have not seen him in some time. Is he well?" she asked, hopping on top of an old tractor tire as they walked.

"Most days," Juniper told her. Then she twisted her face up, using her wondering look. "I don't think he likes his birthday, though. He holds his head and keeps asking if a mystery is here."

Juniper didn't know if cats could smile, but she was pretty sure Story did just then.

"Not *a* mystery," Story told her, "but Mystery. Mystery's my brother. I've come in his stead to see poor Sir Bannendworp."

Rounding a corner the pair came upon a busted down ancient-looking RV that was surrounded by old car parts. There was a golden goose painted above the door, and a suit of shiny armor stood empty, a hollow sentry, just to the left.

Juniper gave three particular knocks on the door three times. A woman, smaller and thinner than even Juniper, with large, wide-set eyes opened the door.

"Juniper, so glad you could make it!" the woman said.

"Hello W," Juniper said, following the woman into the RV and introducing her to Story.

W led the two back into the RV's living area. Old books and magazines were stacked all over. Story saw Juniper place her Cherry Coke in front of a young man with long, grizzled dark hair, who appeared to be blind, seated at a table. A lone candle stood lit before him.

"Oh, Juniper, greetings! Thank you ever so much for coming. I'll enjoy your wonderful gift later," the man said, feeling for the bottle of soda. "I hear you've brought a guest."

"Hello, Ian," Story spoke.

The man named Ian sat back, quickly inhaling.

"Story?" he said.

"I'm here." The cat replied.

"Who's Ian?" Juniper asked.

"He's me." Ian replied, "Ian Bannendworp. No one's called me Ian in years. But, wait," Ian sat back up quickly, "if *you're* here, then . . ."

"Then your birthday wish those many years ago came true, and my brother's work is done. Your past is no longer shrouded in the unknown, but has become a tale instead," Story hopped onto the table in front of him. "And tales, as you know, are my domain."

"I don't understand." Juniper sat down on the floor and crossed her legs, minding a pile of books as W joined her.

"You see, Juniper, Sir Bannendworp and I know each other from a long time ago." Story explained, "Who he is was lost to him in crossing over to this world and, once upon a time, he wished that my brother might help him. This is what came of that wish."

Story sat, staring into the flame of the candle. As Story began to speak, Juniper noticed her voice sounded different; more like Juniper's teacher's voice when she read the class a book.

"In the realm of Bellacree, across the narrow sea

Lays the Kingdom of Yurn.

A nation beyond dreaming, its white towers gleaming

And where time doesn't turn.

But internal strife arose, and not one hero rose

The land, to ruin, fell.

To each surviving member, they couldn't remember

The lives they'd known so well.

In their immortality, they crossed the narrow sea

Where's the Kingdom of Yurn?

With the story now ended, your memory mended

To home, you may return."

The young knight shook his head as if out of a daze. He looked around the room with fresh sight. When his eyes landed on Juniper, he smiled.

"You've been a good friend, Juniper," he told her, "but it's time I leave. I'm long overdue, I'm afraid." He turned to Story. "Thank you, Story. And be sure to thank your brother. You will see that Juniper gets home safely?"

"Of course." Story said as she stood again.

Juniper didn't understand what was happening. Before she knew it, she and Story were the only ones left in the junkyard. W had disappeared into a blue light with Sir Bannendworp.

Story walked Juniper back home, all the way to the edge of her yard.

"Will you be okay?" the cat asked her.

Juniper thought about it for a little while.

"I think so." She said.

"What will you do next?" Story purred.

"I dunno. Maybe I'll go visit the Kingdom of Yurn."

The Books Are Secure

"Its entire west wing is a library!" came a young boy's voice from the back seat. "The Fell Hotel is awesome!"

"I thought you'd enjoy it." smiled his mother from behind the steering wheel.

The young boy, Gregory, beamed as he started reading the pamphlet once more, from the beginning. His mother, Janice, watched the road ahead, silently going over her plan.

*   *

*

"You're in Room 217," said Jacobi Fell, owner of The Fell Hotel. He handed Janice her room key, a knowing smile on his face.

"Thanks," Janice replied, hesitating only slightly. She was a professional. So why was she feeling as nervous as she had her first time?

"I can have your bags brought up if you'd like to get started?" Jacobi's smile warmed.

"Wh-what?" Janice swallowed hard, steadying her nerves.

"The library, Mom!" Gregory insisted, pulling her arm.

"Thank you, yes please." She returned the man's smile.

The library in The Fell Hotel was amazingly expansive for being privately owned. Four floors of books, charts, and antiquities. It was the latter that had brought Janice, as legend had it that this hotel was the final resting place of The Scope of Panthea, a trinket of ancient Akkadian lore for which her client was paying an absurd amount of money.

Having deposited Gregory behind a small mountain range of books, Janice set out on her mission.

Recounting the steps of the plan, Janice noticed a hawk-faced woman, with skin the color of tea, staring at her at the end of the aisle. Janice, her peaceful smile going unreturned by the woman, settled into action regardless.

"Third floor, Ancient Egypt section." She thought to herself, climbing the stairs nonchalantly. "Just need to make sure it's there and come back tonight."

She continued climbing the stairs. Three minutes. Ten. Thirty-five. Frantically counting each step as time ticked. She stopped counting at 347 steps, wide-eyed, and tried to turn back the way she'd come. Three minutes. Ten. Thirty-five. Unable to find her way again, madness setting in, she screamed her throat raw.

*   *

*

"Clio," Jacobi quietly called, standing next to the hawk-faced woman as both overlooked Janice, who was sobbing, frozen on the third step from the floor, not some twenty feet from where she'd left her son. "Let this one go."

"And why should I do that, Mr. Fell? I'm well within my rights. I've broken no oaths."

"That's true." Jacobi agreed, "But that one is one of yours, is he not?" He nodded toward Gregory who was fully absorbed in a lengthy volume about volcanoes. "Shame to make him an orphan. Wreaks havoc on the studies, so I hear."

"Sigh. Fine. But she's going back to their room with no recollection of why she came. And a migraine. The boy can stay. Have someone bring him ice cream."

Janice stepped back down to the floor, wiping tears from her eyes brought on by a terrible headache. She excused herself to Gregory and went to lie down. Clio returned to her scrolls as Jacobi eyed the boy behind the books.

"Now," Jacobi wondered aloud. "Is he a Mint Chocolate Chip or a Tin Roof Sundae kind of lad?"

<u>On a Message Board In Old Town</u>

Too many are the festivals and days of celebration in Timberhaven, especially in the summer and fall. Yesterday I listened to Gaelic harvest music while shopping for African celestial poetry and drinking a masala chai brewed in a Narnian Oathkeeper teapot.

Later, I found a bookseller who had the diary of a tenth-century honeycomb maiden amongst her wares, but alas, I was out of funds.

It's too much going on, I tell you.

<u>Overheard In Old Town</u>

Unless your name is Sherlock Holmes, your perception of things is rarely, if ever, one hundred percent accurate.

Take Gavin for instance. See him over there? No, lower. He's that muddy sand-colored golden retriever lazing by the $hop & $ave's loading dock.

Just a long-in-the-tooth dog taking comfort from the bay door heater, right? You may even feel a little sorry for the old man. Might wanna take him home for a hot meal and some warm snuggles.

Look closer.

Notice how he never really takes his eyes off of that hot dog truck across the street? You think he's ironic?

It's a stakeout. Gavin's a deputy in the Backyard Custodians, an agency of Timberhaven designed to maintain order among the non-biped travelers coming through town. Keep everyone within this reality's construct on the same agreed-upon perception: only human stories can act like humans this side of The Barrier.

And the hot dog vendor that never comes out of the van? She's an emu. Now, I don't know a lot about emus, but I know they typically don't deal in processed meats.

Ah, it looks like something spooked the emu. There she goes. Easy on your tires, love! Bet we don't see that truck parked around here anymore. Too bad. I kinda crave a foot long now.

You come through Timberhaven, take a second glance with your eyes wide open. That's all I'm sayin'.

<u>You Are Cordially Invited</u>

A bashful half-moon lit the event alongside nearly a billion stars. Bullfrogs kept the beat while cicadas played a chorus.

Audrey Fell attended the affair in a gown made of fresh daffodils and sewn river moss. Her first dance was a waltz, her partner an elfin prince who had an unpronounceable name. Then she shared a Hungarian gypsy dance with a westerly wind.

The cake was made from honeysuckle and elderberries, for obvious reasons given the bride and groom.

It is said that the faerie folk prefer fall weddings most of all; at night, amongst the trees. As such, their magicks prove tender in accompaniment of the vows.

<u>Minus Robin's Other Merry Men</u>

Fall Festival was in full swing.

The Friar from Aldfield walked barefoot and plump, in dusty robes and good humor, amidst the crowd of The Village. Honeyed mead and spiced meats were his quests.

He'd brought faded coins pilfered from gilded coffers to barter with, and olden songs from yesteryear if they wouldn't do.

The Friar, having found his necessities, sat down at a table with a guitar player from Fernie and a poet from Cairo. He had traveled far, as all favored fiction must, and was pleased with the respite in such company.

<u>Knowing Your Craft</u>

Hollis Weatherstaff was a magician. Not of the potions and spellcraft type (though his wife Yvainne dabbled in the odd tincture, as was known around The Village), nor was he counted amongst the street mages of Gillencourt Terrace, they with their prestidigitation techniques.

No, Hollis dealt in woodworking.

His wooden toys, puzzle boxes, and decorative carvings drew attention from around the world. (He'd had the distinct pleasure of making gifts over the years for various royalty, two Popes, and once even a Belgian astronaut.)

It was the first day of autumn, and Hollis was walking Duchess Pass in the northern woods. He'd been eyeing a maple tree there with plans to make an elaborate chess set.

As he approached his goal, he heard an angry voice — part growl, part throaty whisper — from within its branches say, "Steer clear of marked tree, woodsman, lest this serve as the end of your tale."

Hollis stopped. He looked up into the maple for the owner of the voice, setting his ax down to appear less threatening.

"I mean you no harm, nor your home," Hollis explained. "I'll happily find another tree." Hollis made to leave.

"What would you make of it, this tree?" the voice came back.

"Hmm," Hollis pondered, scratching his chin in pretend thought. "Maybe a chest. Oh! Or a doll. It could make a fine fleet of toy ships, or. . ."

"This doll," the voice was thick with emotion. "Its arms would work; its legs?"

"Of course," Hollis answered, lifting his ax. "Shall I begin?"

"Aye," was all the voice said.

Tree grims were notoriously malevolent creatures, Hollis knew, if not overly clever. They were spirits from another realm, formless in the real world. Mere seedlings that tried to gain anchor, they occasionally found purchase in trees but all the while sought further mobility in wildlife or the hapless passerby. To leave one living in the northern woods would prove dangerous to others. But to give it a body of its own?

Hollis Weatherstaff had other ideas.

As Hollis cut and fell the maple, the tree grim remained content, almost helpful. It made the chore easy on Hollis, bending the tree to its will. It was only after Hollis had properly sorted the tree and begun carving that the tree grim realized its mistake. Its dark spirit twisted and raged as Hollis carved and cut, causing him to nick his thumb here, slice his palm there.

The tree grim only quieted when Hollis finished his work. A puzzle box, within a puzzle box, within a puzzle box, within a puzzle box. Some of his most exceptional work and a fitting prison, Hollis thought.

"That one is beautiful," Yvainne said from over Hollis' shoulder as he finished staining the large, intricate box.

"Thank you, love," Hollis said, standing. "A pity we can't sell it. Ah well, into the attic with the others."

<u>Audrey Fell Considers Mystery the Cat and His Strange Friend, Penrose</u>

It was early Tuesday morning at the Fell hotel. Audrey, daughter of the hotel's proprietor, Jacobi Fell, had just finished dying her hair and was watching as it dripped crimson into the white porcelain sink. As the dye swirled down, down, down Audrey imagined that the sun rising outside was being born from her drain. She liked the idea that she had lent a hand to the hue of the morning sky through today's choice of hair color.

Audrey leaned over the sink, took the pitcher of water from the counter and rinsed out her hair. Once she saw it rinsing clear, she ran her hands through her hair, forcing out the excess water. As Audrey stood up straight again, glancing in the bathroom mirror, she caught a gray cat peering in at her from outside the window. Not so much at her, Audrey noted, as through her.

Audrey walked over to the window, tying her robe tight around her as she went. It was a peculiar thing, this gray cat. Not only for being outside a seven-story window, but that it paid no attention to Audrey as she approached the window, instead keeping its focus on the space where Audrey had been. Knowing that cats mind what they want to, and not wishing to judge, Audrey simply opened the window.

"You, my friend, are quite the daredevil. How did you –" Audrey began, kneeling before the opened window. The cat seemed dismissive and merely jumped inside, ignoring Audrey's half-asked question. Audrey looked out the window. There was no balcony on this side of the hotel, only the narrowest of ledges along the width of her window. Audrey turned her gaze to follow her feline guest across the length of her room and into the bathroom. The cat jumped up onto the bathroom counter and peered into the mirror.

"Ah, you've found your reflection have you?" Audrey said as she picked up a towel to finish drying her hair, "Not to worry. It's not another cat competing for your territory."

The gray cat turned to look at Audrey as if to say *Thanks for that. Having been born sometime in the last half hour amidst hotel refuse and howler monkeys, I am, as you know, exceptionally dimwitted* and turned its focus back to the mirror.

"Well, excuse me, Mr. Gray, for butting in. I'll go get dressed and leave you to your, whatever it is that you're doing." Audrey said as she left the bathroom. The cat's eyes, seemingly mesmerized, slowly swished back and forth, back and forth in the mirror.

Audrey threw on a pair of jeans and a t-shirt, her typical nice weather outfit. Today's shirt was ratty and torn, and read *Roe and Jules: A Timberhaven High School Senior Class Production*, on the back. High school was over, but a well-worn shirt is its own treasure. It had splotches of paint scattered here and there, giving Audrey the look of someone who'd witnessed a finger-painting incident gone horribly awry.

*   *

*

The man, known only as Penrose, was decked out in a canary-yellow, long-sleeved shirt and dirty blue jeans. He was doing a soft shoe across Maple Street to a tune whose musical accompaniment existed only in his head. He was holding a little white paper bag and mumbling "da ta-da, da ta-da, da ta-da" to himself as his feet did their thing, his hands keeping the beat on nonexistent cymbals.

A car screeched to a halt, stopping just short of hitting the dancing man, as its driver honked the horn and cursed at Penrose. Penrose, for his part, only did a quick turn and continued to soft shoe backward across the street in front of the car; tipping his imaginary hat to the driver with a smile. His white teeth against his dark skin gave Penrose a Cheshire likeness that served to cool the temper of the driver suddenly, leaving the man behind the wheel smiling at Penrose in return.

As he reached the sidewalk, Penrose hummed an old tune not heard aloud in probably a hundred years. He couldn't recall any of the words to it, but Penrose liked to think that tunes changed lyrics like people change socks. It was the music that was the soul of the thing, and that this particular soul wouldn't mind so much if Penrose couldn't remember what color socks it had worn a century before.

Penrose crinkled the bag in his hands, the smile on his face grew larger. "Mystery won't know what to do with his self, once he sees what I found for him." He continued to crinkle the little white bag. The action had, over the years, become the traditional dinner bell between Penrose and Mystery, his traveling companion and friend. Penrose continued to "da ta-da, da ta-da, da ta-da" down Maple Street.

*   *

*

Audrey pulled her newly colored hair into a twisted handful and pinned it up, leaving loose strands of hair sticking out here and there. Mystery sat on her bed, seemingly very bored with the whole production.

"Gave up on the bathroom mirror, did you?" Audrey asked her guest, "You're a peculiar one; I'll give you that. Even for a cat." Audrey gave a quick laugh at her rhyming skills, grabbed her bag and headed to leave, turning toward Mystery as she opened the door.

"Is good sir prepared to make away?" she asked.

Mystery hopped gracefully off the bed and headed out the door into the mirrored hallway, subtly raising his nose as he passed Audrey to signify that he was above such silly antics as playing the role of Good Sir. If anything, at a minimum, he was a Lord.

Suddenly, Mystery darted down the hall and around the corner, out of Audrey's line of sight.

"Mystery, wait!" Audrey yelled after him as she hurriedly finished locking her door. Keys in pocket, she ran after the gray cat, only to turn the corner to find an empty hallway. Empty save for the hundreds of Audrey reflections looking back at her from the hall's mirrors.

*   *

*

Since he hadn't found Mystery in any of their typical meeting places, Penrose went back to the little garden where he had stashed their backpack earlier that morning. The pack was a patchwork design, made up mostly of green military canvas, yellow and red tent material – from a traveling circus he and Mystery had run into outside of New Mexico a few years back –

and old, worn out jeans. It was where Penrose kept his and
Mystery's necessities, alongside a few keepsakes from their travels
along the way. Penrose grabbed a piece of beef jerky from the pack
after carefully placing the white paper bag inside.

"Guess it's going to be lunch by my lonesome today." He
said, taking a bite of jerky.

Penrose finished the jerky and wiped his hands off on his
blue jeans. He reached back into the pack and pulled out a deck of
playing cards. The cards read *Hugo's House of Magic* on the back,
in blue and gold lettering above a magician's hat, gloves, and
wand.

Penrose was a huge fan of stage magic. He loved the show,
the craftsmanship that went into it. Hugo was a sleight-of-hand
magician who had a shop in Eureka Springs, Arkansas. Penrose
had saved his prize-winning rose bush while Penrose and Mystery
had been in the area, and Hugo had been so grateful that he let
Penrose have his pick of anything in his store and promised to
show how the trick worked. Penrose liked cards, so he picked them
but asked not to be taught how Hugo did any of his tricks as that

would ruin the wonder of the whole thing. Penrose liked to wonder about the card tricks. Wondering about them is what made it special.

Penrose sat down, cross-legged in the grass between a gardenia bush and a sycamore tree and absently shuffled his cards, looking up at a bluer than blue sky while he did so. Finished, he turned over the top five cards and placed them in front of him. Penrose heard birds singing in the distance. He leaned back and closed his eyes, letting the sun warm him as he hummed along with the birds.

To the sound of Penrose's humming, in the grass in front of him, the Two of Hearts watched intently as the Six of Diamonds and the Nine of Clubs began a contest to see who could do the most somersaults; while the One-Eyed Jack sang a sweet song to a disinterested Queen of Spades.

*   *

*

Jacobi Fell looked up from his desk at the sound of his office door opening. As Audrey walked in Jacobi noticed a puzzled look on her face.

"Rough morning so far?" he asked, getting up to give his daughter a hug hello.

"Just . . . odd." Audrey replied, kissing her father on the cheek. "If anyone happens across a conspicuous-looking gray cat in the hotel today I'll come to take care of it, okay?"

Accustomed to not always understanding what his daughter was talking about, Jacobi merely replied, "I will indeed." as he returned to his desk. "Off to The Village?"

The Village was the nickname for the downtown district that ran the two blocks between Maple and Pershing Streets. It was within walking distance of the hotel, as was most of Timberhaven if one was of a mind to walk. The Village was a collectors tabernacle; a mishmash of artists, performers, and merchants who came together in a society of their own making. A body could find most anything in The Village if they knew where to look.

Audrey looked at her watch. "Oh! Yes, yes I'm heading down now. Wesley has a new painting to show me. He wants my input before sending it off to the auction house. How he can sell his work – imagine, not seeing it ever again! – I'll never understand, but here I go, off to lend a helping hand to see that he gets top dollar for a piece of his soul!" She made to leave for the door. "Need anything while I'm out?"

"Yes," Jacobi told her, "as it turns out I do have a favor to ask. This," he picked up a purple silken towel with a bundle inside of it, "was delivered last evening. By mistake, I imagine, as I don't recall ordering what looks to be a rather antiquated crystal ball."

Audrey picked up the bundled towel and opened it up to look at the crystal. It had a yellow tint to it. "Looks, I don't know, dirty, I guess. Like it's faded. Lost its luster." Audrey said. "Brynne's then, you think?" she asked her father.

"My, my," Jacobi said, peering into the crystal, "It wasn't so yellowed when I looked at it last night. Correct, though, as I also assumed it was Brynne's."

Audrey gathered the crystal up into the towel and put it into her bag. She leaned in to kiss her father's cheek again. "Okay, then, I'll see you tonight."

Audrey opened the door to find Mystery waiting for her.

"Wha – there you are!" she said as she knelt to the great gray cat, "Where did you run off to?"

Mystery's focus was intent on Audrey's bag.

"You ran off on me! What's the matter," Audrey asked, noticing the gray cat's stare at her bag, "you looking for a ride?" As she went to pick Mystery up, however, he spun from her, stopped three paces away and looked back to the bag.

"Okay, fair enough. You don't like being picked up. I can respect that. Just follow along, then, if you like." Audrey turned back and poked her head into her father's office. "Found Mystery again, so no worries there. Bye!"

Jacobi looked at his now-closed office door. "Mystery?" he wondered aloud, shaking his head with a smile.

*   *

*

Penrose enjoyed a pleasant walk at all times it was fair to say, but especially after lunch on a sunshiny afternoon. He wasn't overly concerned about Mystery, his friend tended to keep his own time and would come around whenever he saw fit to, so Penrose thought he'd wander The Village a bit. Look to what the locals had to show and sell. He hadn't been back in Timberhaven for a good, long while, but seemed to remember thinking that the talent here was pretty remarkable.

As Penrose walked along, he took in all the sights and sounds from The Village. Vendors advertising their wears; one kite maker, in particular, caught his attention with a row of brightly colored kites, their bodies stenciled with all manner of mythological creatures. He saw a two-person act performing *Les Miserables* with sock puppets and play dough, and a young lady sitting on an upturned five-gallon-bucket playing *We Are the World* on the violin.

"Excuse me, sir," a young blond boy, no more than twelve and dressed in bib overalls, asked, stopping Penrose with an out held bottle, "have you yet tried *Aunt Francesca's Vanilla Beer?*"

Penrose's eyes lit up. "*Aunt Francesca's Vanilla Beer* you say? That sounds wonderful!" he said, taking the bottle.

"It *is* wonderful!" the boy said, "And only three dollars a bottle! My aunt, that's Aunt Francesca over yonder – wave her hello – my aunt makes it fresh every night before we come to The Village. It's her special recipe! So, what do ya say, mister, care to try a bottle?"

Penrose smiled. "I sure would like to try it! Tell me, do you and your aunt take trades? You see, I haven't any money, but I do have stories. I've got stories by the bushel! Stories from all around the world! Stories with monsters, if you like, or stories with faraway people and places. I could –"

"No money?" the blond kid interrupted, "Listen, guy, I play the part of a country bumpkin to help sell the soda, I'm not really stupid." Grabbing back the bottle, he added, "If you get some money, come back and see me. Nice shirt, by the way." He sneered, walking back to the woman at the Vanilla Beer booth, seemingly Aunt Francesca, and helping her with some customers there in his grinning child persona.

43

Penrose smiled and went back to walking The Village. He couldn't fault the boy for not wanting to take the trade, even if he had made fun of Penrose's favorite canary yellow shirt in the process. The boy's world and that of his aunt's – if she was his Aunt Francesca, which Penrose suspected she was not – ran mostly on money, Penrose knew. Cold, hard cash. The Dollar was the main character in a good deal of Penrose's stories, especially those of his more recently collected tales, and that was okay with Penrose. The Dollar had just as much right to play its part in the stories of the world as did a mucus-eyed horn swallow down in Briar's Gulch. Even if, in Penrose's opinion, the horn swallow made for a much livelier tale.

Regardless, Penrose thought, the taste of *Aunt Francesca's Vanilla Beer* would have to continue to elude him until some other day.

* *

*

Audrey was busy pointing out to Mystery all the various landmarks that one could see on the way from the hotel to The

Village, inattentive to the fact that Mystery was much more interested in her bag than in her knowledge of any nuanced treasures off the city's beaten path. Mystery's eyes never left the bag that was hanging off Audrey's shoulder. The hunter in him kept his breathing controlled; his heart rate steady. Mystery had ignored a tabby's meowed hello from a nearby garden as he and Audrey walked, so entranced was he in the hunt. In truth, though, he probably wouldn't have responded to the tabby in any regard. Mystery had all the friends he cared to.

As they stopped at the crosswalk to cross Maple, Audrey finished her tour. "And here," she raised an arm to indicate the other side of the street, "is The Village. It really is my favorite place in the world. Well, okay, it's tied with the hotel." The light changed, and they continued the trek into The Village.

"We'll look around in a bit, Mystery, I promise, but first I've gotta go see my friend's painting. C'mon, he should be over this way." Mystery followed where Audrey led. "Oh, wait, first I've gotta go see if this is Brynne's crystal. Back this way Mystery!" Audrey made her way through the vendors, saying hellos and wishing good-mornings to a group of artists she knew as she followed a zigzagging path through The Village. Mystery fell back a few steps, uncannily dodging all the feet from the crowd.

After a bit, Audrey realized the cat was not right behind her anymore. "Mystery! Here Mystery!" Audrey yelled as she knelt down, trying to find the gray through the unruly mob of legs behind her. "Oh, now where did he go?" she wondered. "Mystery! Here kitty!"

Suddenly a pair of the legs stopped right in front of Audrey. She looked up to see an older-looking African-American gentleman with salt-and-pepper colored hair and a canary yellow shirt standing in front of her, smiling a broad grin. Audrey felt soothing comfort come from this man's smile; like she was on a great, comfy couch under one of her grandmother's Afghan blankets on a cold, autumn day, with a good book and a cup of cocoa.

"I'm sorry sir," she said to the man, standing up as she did so, "I'm looking for my cat. Well, he's not my cat – not really – I just met him, but he's my friend, well, we're getting on rather well anyway – whenever I know where he's at, that is – and I didn't want him to get hurt in this crowd, so I tried to pick him up and let him ride in my bag since he seemed so interested in it , but he didn't want to be held, so I was looking for him and, well, have you seen a gray cat?"

Penrose's smile widened. "My but you can talk fast! I wouldn't worry about Mystery. He makes his way, even better than you and me." Penrose stuck his hand out for Audrey to shake. "Folks call me Penrose. I'm Mystery's traveling buddy. Him and me, I guess we've probably seen most everything the world has to show a body. I might've guessed Mystery had run off to find a new friend. What's your name?"

Audrey shook Penrose's hand. "You're Mystery's owner?" her eyes widened, "His name actually *is* Mystery? That's wild! He showed up outside my window this morning, seven stories up! I have no idea how he got there, but there he was! And how'd I even know his name is Mystery? It's like magic! Oh, I'm Audrey. Audrey Fell."

"Well, how do you do, Ms. Fell. Very nice to meet you, indeed. But make no mistake, ma'am, nobody owns Mystery. Mystery and me, we're pals is all. As for his being outside your window this morning, so high up, or how you knew his name and all, well ma'am, that's just Mystery's way."

Audrey felt a little better about Mystery's missing but, while she had a million questions for Penrose, she knew she had to do some things first. "Okay, if you think he's alright. I'm headed over to Brynne's tent, the psychic over there. Care to join me?"

"Will do. You lead the way now, Ms. Fell." Penrose said.

"Audrey's fine, no need for the Ms." Audrey laughed, as she headed over to Brynne's tent. It was garish; decorated with what you'd expect to see in front of a psychic's tent if you were in one of the old black and white monster movies from Universal. A sign above the tent read Madame Xaxu and had a picture of a palm with an eye in the center of it. "Her name is Brynne, not Xaxu, and she has some amazing abilities. I don't know why she dresses it up in this crude charade."

"It's like magic tricks!" Penrose said happily, "All this production adds to the wonder of the experience." He ran his fingers along the purple curtains that framed the entranceway into Madame Xaxu's tent.

"Hadn't thought of it that way, I guess," Audrey said, peeking inside the tent. "Let me see if she's in here real quick. Bry – I mean, Madame Xaxu! Are you in?"

The treasures within the tent were many; silk scarves, burning incense and exotic tapestries. Seeing no one there, Audrey stepped in to place the crystal on Brynne's table. But once she pulled it from her bag, she heard a low, bestial growl, coming from deep inside the tent. Audrey flinched at the sound of it, dropping the crystal ball to the ground with a thud. Looking toward where the sound came from, Audrey made out a pair of green eyes in the shadow of the tent.

"Mystery?" she asked the darkness, cautiously leaning forward.

Just as she went to take a step, Penrose's arm reached into the tent and grabbed her back. "Careful now!" he yelled, pulling her outside the tent as it filled with the sounds of angry hissing and crashing. A deep vibration ripped through the air that caused both Penrose and Audrey to fall over. The very ground shook, and a vicious strangled scream came from within the tent. An explosion of blue light tore through the tent's entranceway, followed by a thick, black and yellow smoke that came sneaking out, escaping from any points.

"What the hell!?" a redheaded woman yelled from a booth across the way. She wore a long, low-cut green gown. Her flame red hair and makeup made her look as though she'd stepped from a Celtic dream.

"Brynne – Madam Xaxu – I don't know what's happening! I just, with the crystal, and," Audrey began, trying to put into words what just happened, "I swear I didn't touch anything."

Penrose helped Audrey up while Brynne ran into the tent.

"I don't know that I'd–" Audrey started to tell her.

"I think it's okay now, Ms. Fell," Penrose whispered.

Brynne quickly came back out of the tent.

"I don't – what just happened?" she stammered.

"I'm not sure, but I'll pay for any damages," Audrey explained.

"That's just it." Brynne said, wide-eyed and confused, "After all that, that, racket . . . there's no damage. Nothing's amiss at all except some crystal ball that's shattered on the floor."

"Well, that's what I was saying. You got a package delivered to the hotel by accident, and I was bringing it to you when . . ."

"I never ordered any crystal ball, Audrey."

"Oh." was all Audrey had in her to say. Both women jumped as Penrose started crinkling his little white bag.

"I'm sorry. I didn't mean to scare you. Just figured ol' Mystery might've worked up a powerful hunger. He always needs a bite after hunting a hopper." It didn't take much crinkling before Mystery walked out from the tent, startling Brynne again. The gray cat walked over to Penrose, cool, calm and collected as any cat you've ever seen.

"A hopper, here in Timberhaven?" Audrey asked.

"What's a hopper?" Brynne asked.

51

"Dark creature," Audrey explained. "It jumps from reflective surface to reflective surface until it's ready to pop and come on out into the world in a new, dangerous body."

"Uh, okay." Brynne shrugged.

"I figure Mystery got to this one just in time." Penrose added.

"But," Brynne said, looking back into the tent, "there's nothing here. Not a – nothing."

"Well I guess there wouldn't be, would there." Penrose smiled, pulling a dried apricot out to give to Mystery, who in turn gobbled it up and expected another. "It sure was nice meeting you ladies, but Mystery and I best be on our way now." And with that, Penrose gave a quick nod to Audrey and Brynne, and he and Mystery walked away into the crowd of onlookers.

Feeling inexplicably calmer, Brynne pulled Audrey aside.

"Audrey, I should just chalk this hopper thing up to something that I don't want to know anything more about, right?"

Audrey smiled and waved to Penrose who had turned and done the same, but there was worry in her eyes.

"I've got to talk to dad." Audrey thought. "There are rules about –"

"Who was that very nice man?" Brynne interrupted feeling oddly at ease with everything that had just happened, waving goodbye to Penrose as well, until he and the gray cat were out of sight.

"His name is Penrose. His friend is Mystery. Beyond that, I don't know."

Brynne hooked her arm through Audrey's and smiled.

"Well, a typical day around here I guess." she laughed.

"Not really," Audrey said, worrying about the customary calms before storms. "There are rules."

<u>Overheard In Old Town</u>

His body still lies where it had fallen on the battlefield, millennia ago, in what 'tis now the West'rn Woods. Though the meat of his lifeless husk would have fed the entirety of the forest's inhabitants for generations, none dared even a nibble. Instinctual self-preservation.

Mother Earth consumed what remained once his spirit left him. Varied stones became his armor; dirt and moss his finery.

It is said that in the West'rn Woods one can sometimes hear the groans of Dargoth, the tyrant king of giant lore, beneath the mountain that claimed him. Whether they be still-living snores or his rumbling belly, or the sounds of him fighting out from 'neath his natural tombstone, none can say sure.

But I can say, 'tis best to err on the side o' caution, kiddies. Stay out the West'rn Woods.

It's All In How You Say It

The Pride of Thirteen was a group of like-minded individuals who met on the thirteenth of every month to discuss, what they believed to be, the significance of the number thirteen.

Two math teachers, six numerologists, and one sufferer of triskaidekaphobia (who was in the group mostly to help overcome her fear) comprised The Pride of Thirteen. Ideally, the group would have thirteen members, but so arduous is the screening process that only special someones are granted admittance.

Mary-Beth Davis thought she was that special someone. Tests for membership were only done on a Friday the 13th. That was the rule. Mary-Beth had waited months for the chance.

Nadine, one of the numerologists, explained the test to Mary-Beth.

"You have to repeat a sequence of numbers that I'll give you here, at the entrance of the cave, to another member at the cave's exit. You must repeat the sequence exactly as I give it to you. You get nothing to write this sequence down with and no light to guide your way. Do you wish to proceed?"

Mary-Beth did. She rubbed the charm bracelet at her wrist for luck.

"Here we go," Nadine said. "8, 5, 4, 9, 7, 6, 5, 8, 6, 7, 9, 4. Go."

Mary-Beth walked into the dark cave. It was reasonably easy going at first. She felt her way along the smooth cave walls with nary a stumble, repeating the sequence aloud.

"8, 5, 4, 9, 7, 6, 5, 8, 6, 7, 9, 4."

But somewhere along the way, the sequence began to sound like gibberish to Mary-Beth. She then did a trick she'd learned in grade school.

"85, 49, 76, 58, 67, 94."

After a while though, even that became white noise to her ear.

"854,976...586,794."

Until finally she combined the entire sequence.

"Eight hundred and fifty-four billion, nine hundred and seventy-six million, five hundred and eighty-six thousand, seven hundred and ninety-four!"

Her voice echoed throughout the cavern, repeating the large number, almost like singing a song in rounds.

It was this what summoned the imp. Notoriously difficult to summon, imps, and they never thank you for it if you do.

The Pride of Thirteen waited until the cave quieted of screams before entering. They knew their numbers were still at nine when they found the charm bracelet.

<u>Belief</u>

Lindsey tied her mother's purple scarf around the top of her snowman's head. With the finishing touches now complete, all that was left was to name him.

"I dub thee Wembley Pizza Northstar, a shieldmaiden of Rohan." She proclaimed to the snowman, naming him after her favorite *Fraggle*, food, and nighttime star. She didn't know what a shieldmaiden of Rohan was, really, but Eowyn was her favorite character in *The Lord of the Rings*, so she ran with it.

Lindsey hoped Wembley would keep the monsters that lived in the forest behind her house at bay. She'd built many such guardians in the past but to no avail. Still the monsters came in her dreams. Dark, musty treemen, with gangly, tree branch arms and moldy peach pit eyes.

Little did she know that Wembley had heard her unwhispered prayer for protection.

Later that day, Lindsey and her family headed to celebrate Christmas in Des Moines at her Grandpa's house. In their absence, Wembley stood tall facing the forest.

"None shall enter while I stand." He thought, charcoal briquette eyes scanning the tree line.

First, the crows came, picking at the string of pearls that Lindsey had placed around Wembley's neck, trying in vain to snatch them for an addition to their sparkly things.

"CAW! You'll scare none of us!" A rather large crow boasted. "The sun will have you first! CAW!" Irritated at its inability to steal the prize, it plucked Wembley's right charcoal briquette out, knocking it to the ground.

But Wembley stood.

Then the clouds parted. The air grew warmer. Wembley's purple scarf sagged down over his now empty eye socket as the snow of his self grew wet in the unseasonable breeze.

Still, Wembley stood.

Trash blew across the yard, and a small empty box marked *Amazon* flew into Wembley's left side, sticking in the wet slush.

Wembley stared into the woods with his one good eye, daring any of Lindsey's monsters to show themselves.

"I am Wembley Pizza Northstar, shieldmaiden of Rohan," he spoke toward the dark forest, as the evening sun went down. "By my oath, you will darken this house no more."

Lindsey didn't return until five days later. A freak ice storm had held her family and her in Des Moines. But the first thing she did when she got home was to check on Wembley. To her shock, she found he'd melted down into a small ice wall that divided her yard from the forest. Her mother's purple scarf, soaking wet, lay behind the wall alongside the string of pearls and a frozen shipping box.

Gathering up what pieces of Wembley she had, she went back inside, somehow knowing that there would be no monsters in her dreams that night.

Must Be A Good Book

Calithan walked downstairs reading a book, oblivious of the din from drinkers and New Year well-wishers in his bar.

"Ten!" the partiers yelled as they all watched a large, special-for-the-occasion clock, its second hand ticking closer to 12.

Calithan, never looking up from his book, continued into the crowd without touching a soul (though the atmosphere was raucous), and through a yellow door

"Nueve!"

that entered into a hall of more revelers. He stopped at a table filled with Spanish coffees and took one without looking. The other end of the hall had a green door which led

"Huit!"

to the patio. Having finished his drink, Calithan placed his empty on a tray and absently grabbed a few beignets. Around the corner through the archway

"Saba!"

stood a group watching a silver-blue flame. Calithan

wandered around through

"Shest!"

a snow-covered crowd raising vodka in preparation for

"Pénte!"

that final tick

"Ceithir!"

of the year

"Drei!"

as the Present becomes the Past

"Dalawa!"

by giving way to the Future.

"One! HAPPY NEW YEAR!!!"

The crowd exploded. Those who had willing lips shared a

kiss and those who didn't drank deep from their cups. The

merriment of the room was infectious.

To all but Calithan.

He merely wiped his left hand on a Tender's towel, turned

the page of his book with his right and headed back upstairs.

<u>The Importance of Stories</u>

The Comic Cave stood dark, grasped firmly in the fist of Old Man Winter. Ice clung to the signage outside as though Tennyson, The Cave's proprietor, had carved it from a glacier.

It was hours yet before the store opened, but Tennyson had already shoveled and salted the sidewalk and entranceway.

The responsibilities of a Caretaker are many, particularly when one is in service to Story, as Tennyson is. No Caretaker of a phone booth is he. (Though he is friendly with Bethany, who cares for the lone phone booth in Timberhaven.)

Tennyson manages The Comic Cave in a myriad of multiple dimensions — though he is not known as Tennyson in each, nor is his store always named The Comic Cave.

On some Earths his store rents movies, on others, he sells paperback novels. He runs a shop in 6th century Kyoto on another Earth and is helping prepare the Kama shrines therein. (Kami take a civil discourse with Caretakers, even if Tennyson and his ilk are of the lower echelons of the cosmic order.)

All of this to say that Tennyson is a being of infinite patience and a master of multitasking.

And yet.

The Snowpocalypse, as the weather people have dubbed it, pushed Comic Day, which everyone knows happens on Wednesdays, back two days. A bug in the system, if you will, that was playing havoc with Tennyson's order.

He arranged the bills in his register for the eleventh time. Fluffed the cushions in the lounge. Finally, he turned on his sign and smiled as he did so. OPEN lit to life in the front window. A clarion call in neon red, announcing 'Here there be giants!' to those who knew to look.

The comic books filled the shelves that lined the western wall. Science fiction and superheroes, pretty pictures and plot; each assigned their post alphabetically.

He'd gone with a comic book store here in Timberhaven because, though Tennyson served Story in every reality, across unfashionable dimensions, these were the important stories.

They mattered.

Though their window dressing varied, Tennyson felt there was no better place to begin one's tutelage into the study of heroes.

And villains.

Timberhaven was in for the storm of all storms, and it was coming soon. There was nothing to be done to stop the coming, not anymore, but one could prepare those who would be willing to fight the good fight. He would do his part.

He would be ready.

The mail truck pulled to a stop out front.

<u>The Race</u>

A young woman stood before an old-timey theater ticket kiosk, her well-worn travel pack slung over her shoulder. She adjusted her hijab and smiled at the small feminine figure behind the kiosk's thick glass.

"Mahin Shirazi," the young woman in the hijab spoke, annunciating clearly into the glass's dilapidated speaker. The old technology was in the shape of a cartoon bear's face; something left over from a popular restaurant chain frequented by children in the 80s. "You know who I am, Duraine."

Duraine, the small woman in the kiosk, acted as though she didn't hear Mahin. Her tiny hand hovered over a clipboard, clicking a pen.

"Shirazi, you say?" Whatever innocence was displayed by Duraine's wide eyes was undone by her mischievous grin. "No Shirazi on this list I'm afraid."

"That's enough foolishness, tender," a voice came from behind Duraine, making her jump. *"Let Mahin in and then go earn your keep."*

"Ah, fiddlesticks," Duraine said as the ticket kiosk and all the other theater exterior trappings disappeared to reveal the interior of a standard barroom. She took three steps and then did a front flip up onto the long bar, twisting her gossamer body to land without a sound. "I never get to have any fun when you're here, boss."

"Mahin," a dark-haired man with shocks of silver above his forehead and at his temples was pouring shots at the bar. *"Have a seat. We've time. On the house."*

Mahin walked over and dropped her pack to the floor, taking a seat on a stool. She took in the other inhabitants of the bar as she sipped her drink. It was getting fuller these days. Not a good sign. Various men and women, of all walks of life, filled the room. Most seated alone. Some were laughing, some weeping. One woman seemed angry, sticking her fingers into the hot wax of the candle at her table and flicking the wax off as it dried.

"You look tired," the man said, downing his shot after.

"I've no interest in racing this year if it won't be a challenge."

"Have no fear, Calithan," Mahin grinned. "I'm more than up to the task."

"Good," Calithan said. *"Tender, my sphere."*

Duraine hopped off the bar and was back with a globe of the world made up of actual earth, sky, and sea. It spun, hovering above her hands with a gravity of its own.

"All yours, boss," Duraine said, handing it over.

"Thank you," Calithan took the globe. Lightning flashed in the sky above Aruba as a thunderstorm broke out. *"As last year's winner, I thought we'd go for Jakarta for our Mark this year."*

"That's fine," Mahin nodded and then finished her drink. She reached down for her pack and pulled out the shell of a box turtle, its sole occupant having long since vacated. "This is our Set."

"Interesting," was all Calithan added.

"The usual eighty days, yes?" Mahin stood and gathered her pack.

"Why mess with tradition?" Calithan agreed, coming around the bar and placing the globe before him toward Mahin. He turned to Duraine. *"Tender, what's our Go?"*

Duraine opened a wooden cash register. Currencies of every manner of creation jangled around inside. Reaching in, Duraine pulled out a thimble-sized obsidian nugget and held it up to the pair.

"Fourth century it is," Mahin said as she reached out to the globe.

The racers blinked from the reality of Cal's Bar and the globe spun where they'd stood.

"PLACE YOUR BETS!" Duraine yelled to the onlookers.

*   *

*

Day One

The hooded turtle dined on fine herbs with a curious rabbit under a fallen bridge in Sunda Kelapa (which was Jakarta's name then.) The hooded turtle told of a sacred warren that protected All from giant eels that climbed from the sea. The rabbit repeated the tale to his lifemate later that evening. By the next week, the tale had grown to include a turtle that walked like a woman.

And so it came to be.

Day One

The turtle with the black and silver markings began by slowly but surely making his way down to the docks to find a suitable ship. Sunda Kelapa was a port city after all. Seeing the vessel he wished, the marked turtle bribed a large pelican with the promise of refuse from the ship to carry him aboard. Once on board, the marked turtle waited for the sailors to share a tall tale. It took until the tenth day, for he had nothing but patience, but the marked turtle finally heard the sort of tale he was waiting for – a sailor who swore to have seen a city beneath the sea.

And so the marked turtle followed the telling.

Day Seventeen

The hooded woman – who had been a turtle – traveled by wagon with a group of holy men. She hid her true face and form beneath robes and a tale of sickness and woe. Moved by the tales of such a talented storyteller, the holy men prayed to their gods for this brother in their midst, that he may find an easier path in the next world. The following day the hooded woman, having met the rising sun as a man, stumbled upon a troupe of actors and abandoned the holy men, leaving only robes behind.

Day Forty-Three

The marked turtle had wandered the city of Atlantis for two weeks. He'd found the book that contained the next storied leg of his race on day four, but it had taken another ten days to find a passage that included a spell of transformation, as he'd grown weary of being a turtle. The Atlantean mystic who was studying her spellbook in bed got quite the fright. ***"Apologies,"*** was all the strange man said before grabbing some of her husband's clothes and disappearing.

Day Fifty-Seven

"You play a woman so convincingly!" the playwright had mentioned for the sixth performance in a row. "You must let me write you something."

"Well," the newly-formed woman said demurely beneath her hood. "Now that you mention it I've had some ideas. Let me tell you a story . . ."

Day Sixty-Four

"And there were knights seated at a round table –" the young man explained to his younger brother over ale.

"Finally!" the man in the funny clothes exclaimed, eavesdropping from a shadowed corner. ***"I'm getting somewhere."***

Day Seventy-Six

"It's you, little one, who takes First Chair!" the hooded woman finished her story to the young burro, Alejandro, and his mother in Spanish. "There is no finer singer in Lord Jarboe's choir." Timberhaven came next.

Day Eighty

"Blasted Hermetic Order of the Golden Dawn," Calithan bellowed as he walked into his bar yelling his problems to no one in particular. ***"Do you have any idea the inane babbling – just outright stupidity that I had to endure, waiting for them to predict the end of – she's already here, isn't she."***

"Hi, Calithan," Mahin waved from a corner booth. "Tough go of it, eh?" She smiled.

"Sorry, boss," Duraine grunted, wiping the bar. "She got in yesterday."

Regaining his composure, Calithan slipped behind the bar and grabbed two glasses and a bottle of nondescript alcohol that smelled vaguely of wild berries. He stopped in front of Mahin and filled both glasses.

"Okay, you win. Who are you picking?"

Mahin looked back to the angry woman who was still burning herself with wax and flicking it on the floor when it dried. Nearly three months later and she was still at it.

"Her," Mahin pointed.

"Tender," Calithan motioned to the woman at the candle. *"Clear her tab."*

"But, boss, she owes a lot. She . . ." but Duraine realized that Calithan wasn't listening and gave up her argument. She wiped a spot on the mirror behind the bar clean.

The woman at the candle suddenly stopped glowering. She drew in a measured, steady breath, actually smiled for the first time that Mahin had seen, and slowly dissolved back to the reality from which she had come.

"Well raced, Mahin," Calithan offered, refilling their glasses.

"You as well," Mahin returned.

<u>Help Wanted</u>

Vernon Wrencleft had made up his mind to seek a new line of employment. He'd only had the position as Timberhaven's resident rat-catcher for six days, making him the job's record holder by three, but he had entirely decided.

Enough was enough.

The thing was if one could stick to New Town as an exterminator, the sky was the limit. New houses and chain stores, all wanting their precious pearls pest free and willing to pay top dollar to see it so. Spray here, lay some traps there, it was a fine living.

But in Old Town . . .

On his first day, Vernon was spraying for termites around the grounds of The Fell Hotel. Suddenly, instead of insecticide, colorful bubbles began blowing out of his tank! It was a puzzle, to be sure, but he shrugged it away. Vernon Wrencleft was a man with limited imagination, you see.

By his third day, Vernon was called to a wealthy estate to lay traps. The manor itself was the pride of New Town, but its grand southern garden, which abutted Old Town, was being overrun by rabbits. As he was setting the traps, a young woman's voice called over the garden wall.

"Excuse me, Mr. Wrencleft?"

"Huh?" Vernon mumbled, looking around confused.

"Hi," the voice continued. "I'm Audrey. Um, I just wanted to somewhat, a little bit, warn you. Rumor has it – though it's more than just rumor – that The Warren has claimed this garden. I'm not sure you should be doing what you're doing."

"Huh," Vernon grunted, continuing his work.

The next thing he knew, he was coming to, bound and gagged in the back of his truck with a note pinned to his chest. It read "NO" at the top and "signed" at the bottom, surrounded by fuzzy footprints in yellow paint that was still wet.

Today, day six in his rat-catcher role, Vernon had been called to The Pub in Old Town. It seemed the owner thought that a dragon had made its way up the plumbing from the sewer. Like they sometimes do. A plume of fire shot out of the front window of

The Pub as Vernon parked and got out of his truck.

"Nope." thought Vernon. "I quit."

Take a Seat at the Back

Torrington had been a thin-skinned playwright who was in town for the declaration of the new Art Institute in 1885.

Unbeknownst to him, the smart evening jacket he wore — he had combed the costume tent of a carnival passing by before arriving — had been the ninety-ninth coat owned by Benjamin Disraeli.

In its front left pocket, on a piece of brittle parchment folded small, were instructions on how to enter a secret room in the library in Westminster. (You pulled the copy of *Philosophiæ Naturalis Principia Mathematica.*)

Torrington had come seeking immortality through the arts, and tales told that a spirits merchant in town by the name of Calithan could make his dream reality.

Far fewer people knew of Timberhaven in 1885 than do today. Calithan himself had started the rumor to drum up business, but he sought Shakespeare. He sought Goethe. So, when this playwright of subpar talent came barging into his tavern demanding an audience, Calithan offered a bench.

"***What have you brought as payment?***" queried Calithan once Torrington explained his wishes.

"Name your price," quoth the fool.

Calithan smiled.

"***It is no small measure, securing your demand,***" Calithan said, rising from the bench. "***A King of Tales title is paid for in talent, and you've not enough to purchase a meager peasant's pillow.***"

The heat rose in Torrington's face.

"***But,***" Calithan interrupted his outburst. "***Give me your jacket, and I'll secure your wish, though you may find the form . . . lacking.***"

Torrington smiled, jerking loose the pilfered garment and pitching it at Calithan.

"Agreed," Torrington smile became a smirk. "Now, immortalize me."

To this day, if you're ever in Cal's Bar and you look, there on an old wooden bench at a back table you'll see the name *TORRINGTON* carved.

Rumor has it that if you run your fingers along it, you can hear the faintest scream.

<u>The Coming of Lord Jarboe</u>

It was a sunny spring morning, and Jarboe, lord of Tater Town, sat leaning against a tree. A Northern Oak, to be precise. Lord Jarboe always strived for precision. Not just with music, though primarily there, but with all of life's pathways.

As he sat, his gallon milk jug crown on the ground beside him, Jarboe hummed a Hiroki Kikuta tune and wondered on the opportunistic tendencies of flavored ice cream, though he had none.

"Take for instance pralines and cream," Jarboe suddenly began a spirited exchange with the lowest-hanging branch of his recliner. "A body might be forgiven forgoing supper altogether in sight of a bowl of pralines and cream. It brings a staccatoed piccolo in accompaniment for goodness sake!"

Jarboe stood then, straight, stretching his arms out to his sides. His back popped during the exchange.

"Rum raisin?" he continued, perplexed at the Northern Oak's suggestion. "No, no. Its companion is a long-winded bassoon. Nobody would thank you for that."

It was as Jarboe was bending down to pick up his crown that he heard it, a pained baritone singing voice coming from within the woods beyond.

"What is this?" he asked. "Who is there?"

The sorrowful bellow continued. Jarboe followed toward the soul-shattered notes as a familiar prickling crept down his spine.

Jarboe carefully picked his way through the trees until there before him in a clearing was Amos, a giant black bear that Jarboe knew. There, at the bear's feet, an evident victim of coyotes in the early morning dark was the body of a bear cub. Amos was prodding his young cub's lifeless form with his snout. The baritone voice, the way in which Jarboe perceived this particular black bear, cracked in anguish amidst the mournful tune.

"Oh," Jarboe's throat clicked, his words stuck in his throat. Bile twitched in his stomach. "Oh, Amos, not your boy."

Jarboe reeled, his worldview spinning as though borne of an angry top. The grief of the scene caused him to topple into memory.

Milton McCanse was a brilliant composer. TIME magazine had called him the Mozart of his generation. Genius. Impossibly gifted. He did for orchestra music what Da Vinci did for secret smiles.

Until, when Milton was fifty-five years old, his only son, Timothy, was diagnosed with cancer.

Having a career that had kept him abroad for years, Milton rushed home to be with his son.

Then came the beeping machines. The IVs. The hospital gowns and the needles. The endless waiting between tests and results.

Timothy's optimism abounded throughout. "I've got this, Dad," he'd say. "No worries. The docs know what they're doing. I'll be up on my feet in no time. Let's do some show tunes together like we used to!"

And they sang *Master of the House*, right there in the hospital room. Then *I'm An Ordinary Man*. Milton, in tears, couldn't continue once Timothy started *Finishing the Hat* though, and so his son sang solo, finding a reserve of strength to belt it out so well that he received an ovation from multiple nurses who had come from the hall to listen.

But it was as the flaring light of a falling comet.

Milton would not recover from his son's death.

The rage Milton felt, betrayed by life itself – by hope, by love. Even and especially by music – it burned him to his core, hollowing out all that was Milton McCanse until only the husk of a man remained.

Thus was Jarboe, Lord of Tater Town born.

Jarboe came to sometime later. Amos, the black bear, was gone, as was the body of the little bear cub. Nature tends to the circle of life in vastly superior ways. It's a thought that Milton McCanse might have had if he had found himself sitting in a copse of trees just outside of a clearing in the woods.

"Now, Tin Roof Sundae, that's an entire brass section!"

was what Jarboe was thinking.

Happiness Is Fried Dough

Archibald and Finnegan, brother donut shop owners.

"Brr," Finnegan rubbed his large, hairy arms as he exited their RV home. "It's quite chilly this morning, Arch. Best bring a coat."

From behind him, still in the RV, "Aye, I will, Finn. And yours as well."

The pair walked over to their shop, *The Crepey Cruller*, to start the day. Archibald bakes the donuts – the stars of the show – while Finnegan decorates them and makes a batch of the brothers' famous *Docteur en Chocolat* (rich chocolate milk served with a dollop of French vanilla cream and a pinch of salt).

The shop nearly always opens to a line in waiting. Customers come in search of breakfast, yes, but also to start their days with joy. Each bite of Archibald's donuts contains happiness. Each sip of Finnegan's chocolate concoction, hope.

There's even a sign above the register that reads *Don't Let Hate Sit In Hope's Chair*.

Some mornings, the brothers sing old songs to even older tunes while serving their wares. They'll teach the lyrics to any who'd join along.

There came the point, along about noon, when the brothers closed down for the day. Archibald cleaned his prep space and oven. Finnegan swept the floor and emptied the till, counting the day's take.

"Good turnout today, aye Finn? Lots of folk joining in on the singing." Archibald winked.

"Aye, Arch, t'was at that," Finnegan smiled. "T'was at that."

<u>Subtle Warnings</u>

The bluebird sat quietly, perched upon a statue of Mary Shelley. She watched as some squirrels played "Who Hid the Nuts?" in the otherwise empty courtyard across the way.

Her name – the bluebird's – was DoReMi. At least that's what she was called on her side of The Barrier. Where your new downstairs neighbor, a toad named Yount, had gone to sleep the night before as a shady greengrocer who'd cheated a wizard on the price of radishes.

The side where magic lived.

Which wasn't to say that magic didn't occasionally seep through to this side. DoReMi had seen it happen plenty of times.

Still. She hadn't helped a princess to get dressed in ages. And oh, to outsing an arrogant bard again! DoReMi feared she was getting out of practice.

This side of The Barrier was much different. Species, for instance, stayed to their like. Every instinct was driven by hunger here. Feral. And a rising darkness had everyone, those of air, earth, and even water, on edge.

She supposed she should cross back over to home soon, where things would be safer for her. But she'd been thinking so for over a month now. The rush of excitement, that "Mayhap the hawk will catch me this time, shred and eat me!" thrill that drives an adventure. It was hard for anyone to quit, DoReMi told herself.

Maybe tomorrow.

Aaron Conaway

After the Rain

Eight-year-old Juniper tugged on her long brown ponytail, the *Big Book of Submersibles* open in her lap, as she reread the same paragraph for the third time.

Jake, who was nearing eight, had placed twenty-three pennies into an empty plastic carton – the bottom part of someone's discarded Chinese takeout – and floated it out onto the small pond that had formed from the runoff of Timberhaven's last big rain. He was heaving giant rocks, doing his best to sink the thieving pirates, and falling far short. His blond hair pasted to his forehead with sweat for the effort.

"Juniper, lookit!" he shouted for the tenth time.

Juniper slammed her giant book shut but placed it gently against the tree where she'd been reading. She reached Jake at the pond's edge as he let fly with another big rock, missing the boat again by a large margin. The pirates further riding the waves to freedom.

Juniper looked at the boat for a moment. She noticed that the pennies were beginning to bunch up on its right side in the wake of Jake's "cannonballs." She then bent down to examine the pebbles at her feet as Jake began towing a huge rock, the biggest he'd tried so far, with two hands back over to the water's edge.

"I'll get it this time!" Jake grunted excitedly between gritted teeth.

Just then, having found the perfect little stone, Juniper stood back up, eyed the distance, and let her rock fly. It hit the right side of the carton with enough force that all of the pennies slid over to that side. Now unbalanced, Jake's pirates went to a watery grave.

"Aww." Jake's bottom lip stuck out, but only a little. He let the big rock drop from his muddy hands.

Juniper watched as Jake rinsed his hands off in the pond. She then wondered how she'd feel if someone were to come along behind her and finish one of the experiments she had started in her laboratory.

She decided she wouldn't feel good about it.

"Hey, Jake," Juniper had an idea. "You know that empty two-liter bottle I was saving for my experiments?"

"Yeah?" Jake stood up, excitement edging into his voice. He loved it when Juniper had an idea.

"You wanna go hunt for pirate treasure with our very own submarine?"

<u>Why Michael Couldn't Swap Stories For Figs</u>

Mahin had sought him in Tater Town, his home amongst the garden, but Lord Jarboe had not been there. She left her care package for him – a collection of spices from Eastern Asia, a beautiful beaded bracelet she'd received from a Yoruba poet, and a small stack of paper containing old pieces of music and songs – just inside the front door of his home.

As she made her way around Timberhaven plying her trade, Mahin kept an eye out for Lord Jarboe. She got some scented oils in The Village with a story she'd picked up in Brazil, about a man who escaped a river spirit by using Capoeira.

At lunch, Mahin purchased an apple by way of a dirty limerick. At a quarter to two, she traded a hunting story for two haikus. Still, she'd not seen Lord Jarboe, and she wished very much to speak with him.

No, it wasn't until nearly seven o'clock that evening that Mahin finally stumbled upon him.

There Lord Jarboe was, just inside the forest, standing beneath his gallon milk jug crown with his arms outstretched before a buck deer as though he was conducting a symphony. The buck, wondrously, bobbed its massive antlers in time to Lord Jarboe's gestures.

"Quite well, Franklin, good show." Lord Jarboe beamed.

The deer bowed deeply before Lord Jarboe at the compliment. Then, seemingly catching Mahin's scent, he bolted for the thicker woods.

"I apologize, dâyi," Mahin said, walking closer. "I didn't mean to ruin your rehearsal."

"Mahin!" Lord Jarboe removed his crown and embraced her as a favorite child. "Think no more on it, my dear."

Mahin returned the hug but was unable to wait any longer "I hear many stories, all saying the same thing. That dark tides are due in Timberhaven."

Lord Jarboe's back stiffened. Pulling back, he wrapped his arm through Mahin's.

"We will get to that, my Mahin." he said with sadness in his eyes. "Now, come, come. Tell me of the world."

Arm in arm, the pair walked back toward Tater Town, catching each other up with their exploits all the while, the world a softer place for the telling.

If only for a little while.

You can find out more about the village of Timberhaven at www.aaronconaway.me. Subscribe for upcoming news, contests, and prizes!

www.ingramcontent.com/pod-product-compliance
Lightning Source LLC
Chambersburg PA
CBHW070519130626
46555CB00003B/1290